Happy Halloween!

By Melissa Lagonegro

With The Morehead Collection's

Teenie Halloweenies®

A GOLDEN BOOK · NEW YORK

Text copyright © 2003 by Random House, Inc. Illustrations copyright © 2003 by Morehead, Inc. All rights reserved under International and Pan-American Copyright Conventions. Published in the United States by Golden Books, an imprint of Random House Children's Books, a division of Random House, Inc., New York, and simultaneously in Canada by Random House of Canada Limited, Toronto. Golden Books, A Golden Book, and the G colophon are registered trademarks of Random House, Inc.

Library of Congress Control Number: 2002094146

www.goldenbooks.com

ISBN: 0-375-82532-0

Printed in the United States of America

10 9 8 7 6 5 4 3 2 1

Halloween is a spooky night.

The moon is full and shines so bright.

Children in costumes of all shapes and sizes

Walk through the streets wearing different disguises.

Each creepy critter searches for sweets,

Knocking on doors, calling, "Trick-or-Treat!"

Some wear dresses

And some wear hats,

Some bring their teddies

And some bring black cats.

Some ride on broomsticks

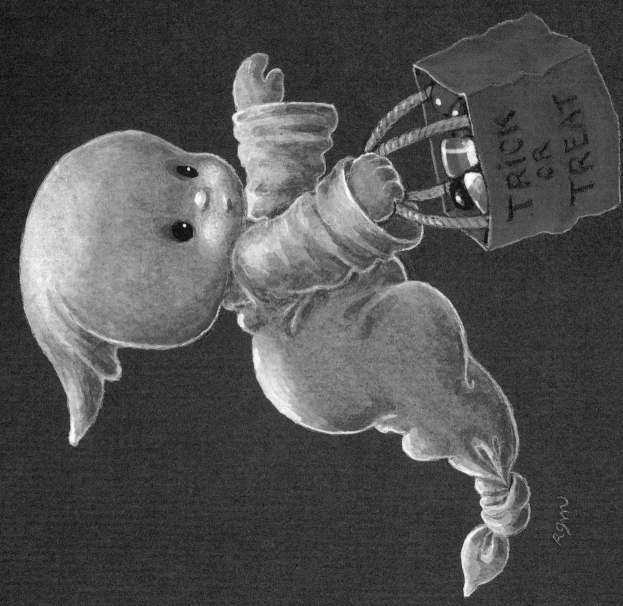

While others float by,

Some walk together

And some try to fly.

There's so much to do on this fun holiday,

Like stuffing a scarecrow with straw and with hay,

Bobbing for apples until someone wins,

Carving your pumpkins with big scary grins,

Joining some friends for a quick game of tag,

And sharing the sweets in your big goodie bag.

With their bags filled with candy,

All the critters that creep

Find someplace cozy
And fall fast asleep.

Happy Halloween!